Finding the Emerald Treasure

Padmaja Raghavan

Special Thanks to . . . .

My parents, my little sister, teachers, and grandparents who thought I could write a story and helped me the whole way through. To my gurus who are teaching and developing me and to the Supreme Lord and savior who is guiding us, protecting all of us.

About the Author

I am Padmaja Raghavan, I was born in Winston-Salem, North Carolina. I wrote this story when I was 9 and a half. Currently I live in Cincinnati, Ohio and I am a 4th grader at Mason Elementary School, Ohio. I loved reading mystery and Adventure books and I thought of a story idea. I have a few amazing friends and when I thought of characters for my story, I quickly included them in my plot. I also love STEM work, art and work on Acrylic and Pencil sketches. Summer holidays and COVID pandemic gave me the time to create an adventure story.

Chapters

Chapter I: A Mysterious Letter.

It was a chilly day, 7:55 in the morning of October 10th, 2020 my friend Sonali, a tall slightly plump girl with short black hair and I were at Nanoclark Elementary, it was the second month into fourth grade, and everyone said the pledge of allegiance. After that when everyone was writing in their planner Ms. Honey a tall slender nice teacher said "Padmaja you are the helper today, please take the attendance to the principal."

So, I put away my supplies, gave the paper to the principal and came back. When I came back everyone was going to the carpet for the morning meeting, I commented to Sonali, "Tomorrow you are the helper".

"Thanks! I almost forgot", She replied.

Sonali and I were good friends for almost 2 years now and we had done a few science projects together. We both have little sisters, and our parents were good friends too, so we get to meet each other often even outside of school.

Throughout recess I was in deep thought about a strange letter I got yesterday evening. Shivering, I turned to try and grab my scarf, gloves, hat, and extra sweater. It was only fall, the frost had already set in, and I was tying my scarf when I realized Sonali was in deep thought too, she hadn't looked right ever since morning and I was curious too, so I asked, "What are you thinking about?".

"A mysterious letter came to my house, it was addressed to me and said that today nobody will be at my home and we will be attacked, it said somebody was going to come and help. But I am not sure who he said would come and explain everything." Whispered Sonali worriedly.

"I got the same letter" I whispered in reply.

"Do you think it is just a trick?" she doubted.

"I don't think so but if it is that is a pretty mean prank, we can never be sure until we go home though."

Later that day we decided not to pick up the topic of the mysterious letter but when we saw each other we could read each other's mind, on the bus we rode together in silence, when we got off our fingertips became numb and we could see our breath.

We immediately changed pale and turned in different directions. I felt a feeling, it felt like something wrong was going to occur, it is a thought probably only Sonali and I felt. I took 3 deep breaths and closed my eyes.

Everything is gonna be ok" I whispered to myself. Then when we reached our home, we found nobody was there and it wasn't a trick, when I looked in the kitchen, I saw a half-drunk tea and a nibbled sandwich. My mom is the only one who drinks a tea in the afternoon in my house and the chocolate sandwich means my little sister was having a snack. I ran around see if they were around. I couldn't see them, I assumed they may have been kidnapped.... I looked around the house again.

Then I found a piece of paper right there on the ground and it was another mysterious letter that said, "Prepare to meet me at 10:00 pm with your other friend, I will meet you on one of your driveways. I want both of you to stand on the same porch." this one was signed but the name was smudged. Then I ran to Sonali's house & I saw that it was empty just like mine. There she was reading a letter after she had finished reading it, she pursed her lips and wrinkled her eyebrows.

Right then Sonali's dad had been coming into their driveway with Sonali's baby sister in her baby car-seat who was walking out of his car, Sonali and I both told him about the Mysterious letter and the strange incident.

He said "I can give you permission if Padmaja's dad will also give you permission to go out and wait to see who wrote those letters and what is going on" that is when I realized my dad would have been home by now as well!

So, I raced to my house and explained everything to my dad. He was perplexed, anxious and then calmed down as I explained. "Yes, I will permit you and Sonali to go but stay at the same location as the letter mentioned, ah! There is an idea, invite Sonali to dinner!"

"That is a great idea" I remarked, so I called Sonali on the phone and invited her to dinner. She was allowed to come to my house for dinner that night. Her dad also agreed to come and discuss the matter. I didn't know it then, but this would be the last dinner I would have with them in a long time. At dinner everyone was talking about the mystery. With the moms of the houses missing, dinner was the not the best as we wanted to enjoy, but the purpose was well served. The dad's talked, wondered, and suggested a few ideas. I wasn't sure if we should be calling the police and Sonali and I thought about that as well. My dad and Sonali's looked at the footage of the camera in the front door and the back, they looked at the doorbell camera videos as well. They didn't find any mystery. There was no one at the house the whole day except the mailman and an Amazon package drop off at Sonali's door. This was becoming a bit of an unexplained mystery to us. I told my dad not to sneak behind us as we waited in the driveway. That night Sonali and I stood waiting for the person to pull up into my driveway in a car, but at 10:00 pm we both saw a snow-white Pegasus swoop down and took us with it before we could even say goodbye to our parents!

"Wait! Stop! Come back" our fathers cried.

Chapter II: Off to Save the Universe

A pitch-black figure was in front of us.   We were shocked!

There was not much time to introduce or get acquainted. As we saw some moon shine on his face, we figured it was a boy and the white shining Pegasus was blinding us.

"I am Shriyan, our kingdom is beyond the 3 seas and the 12 rivers, whatever happened to your home happened to that kingdom, my father is the king of Celestiopia and I am the prince of the land. He attacked your houses and my kingdom and took the people as prisoners, but I have no idea why! The Emerald is told to give someone untold powers, but if that happens there will be a terrible price to pay", Shriyan told us in a hurried voice.

"Who is he and if he wants the emerald why does he need your kingdom and our parents?" Sonali asked. "The shape shifters I think, want to rule the world with his monsters and snake armies. Sorry if this wasn't clear, but we have to go fast, they are very quick and can find the Mysterious Map leading to the emerald easily in a maximum of one earth week! He has sent out troops to find the Mysterious map leading to the emerald".

"What's with the Pegasus? I have seen horses but not winged horses", I asked.

"To get across the 3 seas and 12 rivers faster. Ah, here we are, we will cross the seas and rivers here" Shiryan replied. After a few hours of sleep, it was 7 am.

Shriyan quickly asked us "We will be attacked by monsters so which weapon would you like?". We woke startled from sleep.

"Bow and Arrows for me "I replied.

"Same with me" Sonali.

"You know how to use a bow and arrow?" we doubted at the same time, we giggled.

Then Shriyan handed us both golden sword and said, "These magic swords can kill the monsters in case something happens to the bow and arrows and until we get your weapons, I will also be using a bow and arrow, beyond the 3 seas and 12 rivers, we will get magical bows and a quiver which will never empty later in our journey". Shriyan Mentioned. ¨We must cross the river and seas to start our journey first¨

Chapter III: Our First Battle

After a couple of hours in silence there was a loud bang! We all stared in astonishment, holding our breaths we carefully examined the land underneath us and in about 5 minutes or so thousands of snakes and monsters attacked from all sides. Using our swords, we killed most of them and injured some. Then the breathless we kept going on, there were still 3 or 4 snakes left, it was our last shot! After a few minutes, the snakes from the Serpent king army sprayed some venom on us. Shriyan quickly fended them off. We fell to the ground unconscious. When we all were revived from the venom's effect, Shriyan, Sonali and I drank some of the medicine that Shriyan kept in his saddle bag. Later that morning Shriyan, Sonali and I had become great friends. We had been talking and getting to know each other.

Sonali asked if we would be having luncheon at noon but Shriyan reminded us that food was scarce and so was water on this dangerous journey but gave us each a piece of flatbread and a few cooked vegetables, we all tried to act like nothing was wrong but no matter how hard we tried, everyone knew that everyone else was worried we were starved, and thirsty with a dry throat so Shriyan gave us each just a sip of water, that was the price we had to pay to save the world. I hoped this was a dream, or a fairy tale or just a false alarm but it wasn't and I knew it. It is hard to deal with cold hard facts!

Chapter IV: Doomed!!

We were passing through the sea when the oceans all joined and made a huge storm, and many were there at the same time. There were hurricanes, tsunamis, and many of them too. There was hail and snow and thunderstorms too! There was even lightning, and I was scared because water conducts electricity and so do, we! We were washed away into the sea (I guess we fainted or became sick when I tried to get back to an island. I thought I saw Shriyan as a mythical sea creature and the next minute I didn't.

Chapter V: To the Rescue

I didn't know what happened for a long time I guess and I assume we became unconscious and the next thing I remember is that a soft, sweet voice came across us and then Shriyan was trying to wake us up, we had crossed all of the rivers except 2 and we had crossed all 3 oceans.

Sonali and I met a new set of creatures they were called dolphorons and could be on sea land or sky, but they had to know they had that power, apparently Shriyan's mother was the Queen of the dolphorons and the only reason the serpent hasn't bothered these guys is because they can attack from anywhere and are more powerful, but he doesn't know their weaknesses!

"You are part of the long lasting dolphoron dynasty" Shriyan's mother said regally we suddenly turned into the swimming version of them "Why do we need the Pegasus then?" I asked "Because we need to carry things and two is that we would wear ourselves out since we are travelling such a long distance" Sonali and I were still in shock, we had so much info to digest in!

At dusk we ran into a huge pool of molten lava and for some reason we swam through it. To our surprise we had not any wounds! Not even a burn! Then smack in our faces the huge mountain popped up and we swam around it. When I came out, I asked Shriyan if that place where we met the dolphorons was the 11th river and he replied "Yes! Actually, all the rivers are their property except the 12th river".

"Wow that was a pretty big popularity of dolphorons we saw" Sonali exclaimed.

"Why can't we just fly above these rivers the dolphorons own?" I questioned.

"Good question, my mother told me you would ask this, well there was a very old curse which states that any creature flying over this area will burn to ashes." He replied with a sigh.

"Oh, well at least we came this far!" Sonali said looking at the bright side.

"Hey where is the Pegasus?" Sonali and I asked in unity.

"Well, when I tap my wrist 3 time he will magically appear before me but underwater he will drown so we must find land first".

Chapter VI: Seeing True Magic

At dawn the next day, we found a change in the water and that is where one of Shriyan's dolphoron cousins told us to get out, when we had all got out our clothes turned dry and by that time Shriyan had activated the signal and Snowbright (I now named the Pegasus that) had appeared. We reached a large river from which we drank to our heart's content, as the moonlight gleamed and shimmered in the freshwater, we saw many gorgeous flowers bloom and lighten the surroundings of the river. They were the most beautiful lily like flower I have ever seen, "What are those beautiful flowers?" Sonali and I doubted

"Those are the moon flowers, they glow only on the full moon, it is said that" and before Shriyan could finish , the

Pegasus dived down and then it seemed as if it was gliding on the waters of the river. I was able to grab a handful of the flowers and it felt magical as if it told me something. I held them not tightly but gently and I put them in my pockets and thought about it for a moment. That is when I realized this was actually the 12th river and I couldn't believe that we had come here so fast, it was due to the Pegasus, because it was from a different world.

I whispered, "these are magical flowers that could help us through the way". I told them how I felt and how it made me feel that it could help us fix this mess! They nodded in agreement, and just before we could finish nodding the wind blew cold, so cold that in one puff our hand went numb. We shivered in the coolness of the air. I felt like I was about to freeze into ice, and I knew my friends felt like that too, but just as the wind swept us the second time full moon reflected on the water. In a flash a beautiful woman, who had shimmering eyes and her body and gown were silver-white appeared in front of us and after we had all recovered from shock of the cold and a magical flying woman she started speaking in a sweet voice

"I will give you all strength to help you all to do whatever you want to do, so will the sun and Canopus, down that path through the forest of monsters lies your next step, down there will be many different monsters but that is the path for you three". She smiled.

"Who are you and is this your river?" I asked.

"The maiden of the moon of course and yes this is my river made by my magical moon liquid and since you drank it, now you have some extra strength". "Oh, and one more thing!

Take a moon flower each and make sure it glows, make sure it is bioluminescent and a little flamboyant. I will invest some of my power in this and will help you overcome many of the obstacles that come your way" and saying that she disappeared into the moon. We decided to take some of the magic moon liquid for when we might need it so Shriyan took out a large empty canteen that he had in his saddle bag and took as much as we could in it. We closed it tightly, so none spills out. After that Shriyan kept the canteen back in his saddle bag, both the canteen and the bag were really large. Shriyan said he had one more bag which had medicines that were made with special herbs found only in the Hills of Tranquility. Also, another canteen for other things we might need, then it had water and the other saddle bag had some flat bread and some cooked vegetables for the journey. I think he probably took big ones from his kingdom so that we can store and save as much as we can on this journey.

Chapter VII: The Adventure Just Begins

As we entered the forest, I started to get a feeling to always hold on to my sword, so I reached my hand for the sword and clenched my fingers on the sword, that is when a Trio of witches had come our way at that moment.

I had hoped they were nice witches, but their rugged voices gave us a frightening warning "When you least expect it, we'll be there. Why don't we magic you in the sphinx pyramid?"

"That's an idea" cackled the 3rd witch.

"I wanna do it" whined the 2nd witch and before we knew it, all the 3 witches had done something (I don't know if they are witches, they just looked like that) we were in a magic pyramid and we thudded onto the ground.

Chapter VIII: A Conundrum!

"Mwa-ha ha that's right no flying here Missy, and for you boy" she snapped. She clapped her hands, and he was tied and was drowning into a bubbling green liquid, boy! that was flamboyant. That place looked so antediluvian with cobwebs and dust everywhere.

"Let me go!" he cried.

"Ok, if you want to save yourselves then your friends have to solve this riddle, I give you" she hissed.

"ok let's do it" Sonali said hurriedly I nodded in agreement.

"What do all animals in zoos want the most? "she snared at our confused faces. Suddenly I knew the answer.

"FREEDOM" I cried. Growling she set one more challenge.

"You managed to break my no-fly spell but this time you will never be able to escape!"

"ok will do it but if we pass, we will get Shiyan back" we both replied, "fine if you pass you save him if you fail you all drown and I will have some lunch after a thousand years", she snickered. "You must save the boy from the drowning on this bridge, blindfolded also with many obstacles in your way". That is when we realized that Shriyan was going to drown in about 5 minutes, and so guided by Shriyan's voice, we started crossing the bridge, when spears came at us. we heard the sound of the old pyramid crack, so we were able to swiftly dodge them, quickly. Sonali untied and freed him in time so that he wouldn't fall, he thanked us, and we hopped on out. The Sphinx roared.

Then we realized we didn't know where we were and which way to go. Luckily an incredibly old blind monster that thought we were young monsters and told us the way out, so we dashed out on the top of the Pegasus". Are those also part of the army of the ShapeShifters?" I doubted.

"Yes, those creatures are part of the army but that is the last part of his army" Shriyan replied.

"How did you know we needed help and how did you get into our world from your world and still survive the climate and changes?" Sonali asked him.

"Well after the Shapeshifters had kidnapped my kingdom, I followed him and that is when I left those notes. The surviving part happens when we go at a certain velocity on a certain trajectory so we can escape the gravitational pull of the different worlds." We listened in awe. So, we rode on a Pegasus.

Chapter X: A Horse Hassle

When we got to where we thought the Mysterious Map was, we saw a note. Meanwhile Shriyan was nervous thinking the "villains" got it. But when I read the paper aloud it said "Beyond the deepest and darkest seas, the jewel lies there, guarded by the black sea. If you are to find it, you must pass through the River Well Village first then you will find the Mysterious Map leading to the emerald of untold powers".

Shriyan was relieved and he spoke.

"Don't leave it here. The serpent will find it, so take it". But when the note was brought on Snowbright, it started going crazy as if it knew what it meant, and I felt as if I could understand it.

For a minute I thought I was crazy, but it talked to me, it said "I am the horse of the moon, she will help you. I know where to go, this is the magical note. We must go to the River well village, find the map, which leads to the black sea, then cross the black sea and it will be a success, nobody has crossed it, and nobody has survived before. Across it is the emerald, after you have that, the moon will help me cross over and I can fly over and get you".

Then I asked aloud, "You can't fly us across the black sea?"

"No" he replied. Then I realized that my friends were staring at me.

"Were you just talking to Snowbright" Sonali enquired. "Ok, Yes, the moon is connected to me and the Pegasus, we must go to the village, find the map and across the black sea and the horse cannot fly us across, so after getting the emerald, the horse will come back, due to a signal from the moon I explained. When you shine the gem in moonlight, sunlight, and starlight it gives you untold power but with a terrible price to pay, we can't let the villains get to it! That will reveal what is needed to defeat the serpent, the horse clued to me, that is all it   said".

After this remark we flew off to River Well Village totally trusting Snowbright, I was completely nuts!

"How old are you?" Sonali questioned Shriyan. The same age as you, he said with a chuckle. By this time, we were very dirty, clothes torn and hair in a mess.

Suddenly Snowbright said, "The Map will show you where the black sea is, since that is a hidden place" said Snowbright.

Chapter XI: Gathering Knowledge

We swiftly reached the village early in the morning. When we landed, Shriyan announced – we had to come here, because there is something precious here. Sonali wondered if this was where we will get our weapons.

"Yes, it is "Shriyan replied with enthusiasm. After a while of looking around and sightseeing we met an old man.

"Come, come! I will tell you some secrets about your mission and give you your weapons" the old man said. "How can we trust you?" I asked. "He is the person we are looking for, the wise man of the lands beyond all your world". Shriyan reassured us.

As we entered his arena he said "The middle snake, the oldest one has a jewel he keeps on his forehead, if each of you can shoot one arrow each on it, he will be defeated. Here are your bows, the moonlight bow for Padmaja, it is light, wields well at the atomic regions its arrows can travel in the dark spaces".

"Who is this snake and what does that have to do with our mission?", Shriyan asked.

"You will find out when you go a little farther in this adventure", said the wise old man.

Chapter XII: REAL Artifacts

He gave me the bow and asked me to focus. I had never seen a bow like this, Light as air, I closed my eyes for a second and felt an inner startle. Starlight bow for Sonali which was blue. She handled it as if she had done this before, as she tied the bow string it lit up and it was supposed to be capable of plunging arrows through gaseous nebulae. Shriyan had the sunlight bow. As Shriyan picked the Bow, the limb bolts and the bow seemed to adjust itself to his comfort. Shriyan looked at our surprised faces and said this is a magical bow. The elements of the celestial world will align themselves with the archer.

The wise man introduced an element of magic every time he said something. "The moon is connected to Padmaja, the star Canopus to Sonali and the sun is connected to me" he declared. We almost started to leave, he said to take our quivers along with the arrows inside it.

Handing us specific moon, star and sun quivers he cautioned us, "You must only use the specified bow with the specific arrows and quivers otherwise the power won't work. Just like the chargers on your specific handheld things on earth. But the quivers don't empty so you will not have to worry about where you will get other magic arrows".

We ran our hands over the quivers, thanked him as we hung it behind us on the shoulder and strapped it tight.

Chapter XIII: Imposter

It had been two days since we had eaten anything like a real meal. There was so much going on and we had hardly felt hungry or thought about it. We went out to get food that is when Shriyan's friend came and offered to help us rest, provide us with food and water, as well as a nice refreshing bath.

Shriyan said to make ourselves at home as the girl about our age had helped us get the bath ready and she poured some rose powder in the bath and after everyone was finished she had treated us to a delicious lunch or dinner I didn't know which one, you see in adventures like these you can't look at the time, you must act like it there was only a minute left, so I looked up into the sky after the meal.

We had all finished lunch and finished chatting for a few minutes. While I was talking to Shriyan, Sonali was with the girl "What is your friend's name?" I asked Sonali and the girl had been talking.

"Her name is Sanvi" he replied. Right then when we were planning on leaving, we couldn't find Sonali or Sanvi, they were talking a second ago, and when we were looking around in a room, we saw Sanvi had a secret doorway to another place "SHE IS AN IMPOSTER!!!" Shriyan yelled.

Chapter XIV: Dimensions

We decided to follow her, but when we were about to enter the secret room a person grabbed us. We quickly turned to see who it was, and to our surprise it was the wizard. He told us that we wouldn't be able to breath in that world and told us that a shape shifter had taken the place of Sanvi and had taken Sonali into the shape shifter world "But there is one way to breath there, it is called *Trophogrophology*". He taught us how to do Trophogrophology. So, we made sure that the food and the canteen of moon liquid from Shriyan's saddle bag is safe so that when we rescue Sonali, she can heal from the breathlessness and we all could rejuvenate and rehydrate. It was time, we set off over the horizon.

We went through the closing portal, At the same time we performed trophogrophology and found ourselves in a different dimension. "This is what you earthlings call *Venus*. At last, we've got the culprit!" Shriyan whispered in my ear.

I nodded in reply, we quickly snuck past the guard when I took some sleeping powder from his bag and sprinkled it on them. Of course, I used a special sleep powder cloth so that I wouldn't feel lightheaded and faint.

We could see some creatures & Sonali in a cell, coughing and trying to hold on. She saw us for a moment and then I think she fell unconscious. We could hear the King of the shapeshifters talk to a woman I think was a Queen. The woman cackled "Now that we captured one of the wimps, the others will be scared off and when the Serpent find the emerald, he promised us a Share of the powers".

"Yes" the King said in a deep and proud voice.

"So, this is what the wise man meant", I whispered.

"Yes" Shriyan whispered back.

"Who is that?", the shapeshifters yelled as they went out of the cell to call a guard to investigate the matter. I couldn't bear it anymore; she was my best friend, so I jumped through the window of the cell and grabbed Sonali. I saw the real Sanvi in the same condition nearby in a corner of the room too. I signaled Shriyan to pick her too and we quickly slipped past the guards, since the sleep powder's effect was still working.

We jumped into the portal and speedily did trophogrophology and quickly poured the Moon liquid into their mouths. It looks like the moon flower helped Sonali hang on. Sanvi explained how they made a spell, so that she would become a black hole starting with a nebula to a star to a Red MegaGiant, then a hypernova, a planetary nebula and then a blackhole, and that the spell only worked in that dimension, she also said that if we hadn't got her then, then she would have been gone forever. "I will stay here and protect this hidden island" Sanvi said as she waved bye.

Chapter XV: Continuing the Journey

When we started flying on Snowbright a very stern and bold voice approached us, it was the sun. I had not seen the bubbling sun so close before. It was hot, burning and bubbling, it was loud, and I could see the magnetic waves plunging in and out of it, but I was not sweating but I could feel its radiance!

The sun approached us like a caressing mother and said, "I will help Shriyan on this mission along with both your friends". We bowed and smiled and continued. A few hours later perhaps. I have no idea of time now. I didn't know if this is space travel but suddenly the Moon appeared, we had seen her before.

She held my hand, kissed my forehead, and said, "I will stand by you, Padmaja".

It was an intense dark sky, with stars and asteroids flying past us, Canopus flew by and said, "I will help Sonali". Seeing Sonali feeling reassured, we held our hands and nodded our heads.

"We have been flying south since I saw Canopus", I thought.

As if Shriyan reads our mind he said, "Yes, south bound".

We flew on Snowbright to a red planet which I guessed was Mars. The trajectory wasn't as difficult as the last one, we just had to fly across the path. Then we saw a huge glowing light, coming from a corner as we walked toward it. We covered our eyes since the light was very blinding and when we reached Olympus Mons the huge dormant Volcano on Mars and on top of it was the Mysterious Map. I just thought, "What would my teacher think of my absence" when Sonali picked up the mysterious map.   A deep Voice came "Get into the next compartment which the Canopus will lead you to the black sea then you will cross it, that will lead you to the place you need to go".

Chapter XVI: The Last Obstacle

The world of the serpent is deep in the south, I guess. We landed on a shore of some place dark and pungent smelling. Snowbright said "The dark seas … I cannot do any further, so I will have to wait here". We could not make out where we were. Like all other meekly earthlings, we saw we had no knowledge of these areas as we were following Shriyan.

Sonali and I didn't know if we were to suggest an idea or go with the flow or question. Extremely perplexed for a minute, my mind was all back at home. How did dad react when he found I didn't return home? Is he ok? My thoughts were abruptly interrupted by a voice of a star. Out of nowhere a star appeared and offered to shine.

It said I will shine by reflection. You can walk over the seas in parts where I shine. You can walk across the seas. I was exhausted to think or thank. I walked where the light shone. Below was a very slimy, dark and gel like sea. Something told me, it would sink anything that fell in. I was careful not to trip. I watched every step I placed on the reflection.

Shiryan seemed to walk easily. Sonali tipped-toed for a while, her toes may have hurt, she started to walk. The star, as if following our thought although leading the path, explained to us that the dark seas are strange waves of unhappily dead stars. Their spirits are grumpy, and they swallow in an unending hunger to regain stardom. I tried to interrupt that this is what we call as blackholes, but guess gravity, the hunger of the star is a mysterious one, my voice was not heard. I tried to recollect what I had learnt, but the star spoke on.

She said there is neither light nor darkness, just jelly waves of dust. It knows neither good nor bad, it's not happy or sad, just in a state of regeneration. She and her other stars of the constellation of Corvus could span this sea easily. One among them, Hydra, had died in a battle to outshine Altair.

We had reached the other side of the dark sea and could see some distant light. Shriyan said Corvi stars are bound to the sun. They help us. Corvi bowed to Shriyan and vanished. The sun appeared again, here are some golden armor, it will come in handy, when we battle the 9 headed Serpent. We took turns staying guard and getting shut eye, Snowbright again knew what to do, he knew we had to go to the asteroid belt.

This time I was on guard and I had least expected anything. The witches appeared; I woke my friends. We pulled our bows. After many magical arrows from all three of us, the witches were defeated. We had not suffered any injuries. The sun almost seemed to follow Shriyan all the time. Or were we circumventing it? I had no idea. I had no sense of direction, there were no GPS signals, no traffic yet many star crossings. Some colliding, some out shining, some collapsing, some detouring, some even funnily making a U-turn and retracing its path.

After viewing the skies on a nightly canvas, to me this was surreal. As every Asteroid or star, we passed, I wished my mom and sister was in it. As much as I missed them, I wanted to know why us? Sonali exclaimed that she doesn't know how long it's been or how much longer it will take but we are on a mission, a mission dear to all three of us. Each with a reason and filled with determination. "We are almost there", replied Shriyan in a haste. He almost got things sped up. He said in one hour we will reach. Something which I cannot see how he measured. The map sped us up. We were hungry again. Sonali asked if she had time for a quick snack. I was thirsty too. Shiryan's face shrunk, we understood that was not the time for a snack or drink but still we ate half of what we had and saved the rest for later.

Shriyan was way different from the kids of our age. He had a sense of time without a watch, direction without maps. He could talk and remain silent yet communicate. His friends and enemies were several years older than him, yet he commanded respect and treated them all with respect.

We were intrigued. He had knowledge of the weapons and the earth and its ways. He acted as if he knew us for many years. His urgency in finding our parents was not difficult to understand. He said his kingdom was in danger and he must save it. He didn't talk much about it afterwards. I didn't ask him either. With just one hour left to reach the battle ground I was tense.

My heart was pounding. I could hear the voices of the celestial beings tell us about the bow, quiver, armor, spells, and promises to come to our rescue. I didn't know their ability, but I was not able to hold my excitement.

On a normal day I would have been in Math and Art class, chatting away in recess and giggling at lunch. I was no longer looking forward to the bus ride with Sonali but the mission to rescue our family with a total stranger. A stranger who knew everything, in fact more than I did about my family and me. I gathered my courage and asked, "Shriyan, why exactly are we in this? What is the connection to your kingdom and our mothers?". Shriyan smiled as if he was happy that we finally asked.

"ah, so 20 minutes to reach, finally after several hours of travel we only now find out our true roles". We were embarrassed. Sonali and I held hands.

Shriyan explained the story of his father and grandfathers being kings and rulers of great reputation in the land of Celestiopia. It is a golden sparkling land where people loved each other, there was plenty to eat and drink. The sun and moon were friends of his father, the great kind king. The emerald is a source of magic and plenty. It gave us peace and happiness. We kept it in the safety of the palace and all people could come and see it.

The evil serpent of the South ruled his planet in the remote constellation. The people in that planet were always raging in anger, never fed food properly, water was scarce and one day it vanished from it. There were no trees or rain. Fire started to burn in many places. Many of the stars thought the planet transformed into one of them. The wise Canopus explained it was not possible for a planet to become a star but vice versa. She also said about how the serpent planet is Saturn as we Earthlings call it.

The planet struggled in between a stage of deep dark seas and a red giant. My father called the council of wise stars and decided to help them by installing the emerald in that land so they can be happy too. The cruel and cunning serpent took the emerald, and along with it my father and mother. With my father gone, we were afraid and confused. The Serpent captured my people and is now in his kingdom. I need to save them. Free my people and my parents. Shriyan finished explaining.

We were shocked. As much as it sounded like a fairy tale it was real, we were with a prince. We hadn't gotten answers to all our questions but were happy we knew some part of the story.

Chapter XVII: The Last Battle

Suddenly the floor cracked in two and we all fell down. A down that never seemed to end, in an endless gravity we sunk but could see some light in the end. We found our families bound and gagged. The nine headed serpent had no armies then. I remembered we had killed some monsters on the way and so were happy he was alone. Sonali and I first drew our swords. The one we held from the time we entered this expedition. Zoom he came in and blasted. We lost them.

Quickly we held tight the bows and reached the quiver over my shoulder. We knew we had to strike, there was no way I could predict which head would do what. I thought let's shower with arrows, we will use my one-time boon of the Sun, Moon, and stars later when he was worn out. We battled long and hard. We were three but he was nine headed and had thrice the advantage. He was spitting venom and fire. We had minor bruises but never got hurt seriously. I could see my mother and sister looking at us. My sister was crying and trying to free herself. The armor worked like a charm and was worth every help by the Sun, Moon and Stars.

Shriyan had a plan, he whispered it to us, we nodded in response. Then he left.

Suddenly the Moon, Sun and Canopus came in and shone so bright, the serpent could not focus. We all had a good aim shot our arrows in unison and hit the gem. He was defeated and succumbed to the magical power of our arrows. The Moon, Sun, and Canopus the star had a forcefield and it worked for us, respectively. We felt all powerful and strong and so much happier than ever. Our mothers were freed. I ran to my sister and hugged her.

Then Sonali and I ran out to help Shriyan, we together carried the emerald and gave it to the King of this land beyond, he smiled at us.

I thought the armor would go away after the battle and the serpent lay bare. It did not. After a few hugs and happy exchange of glances. Shriyan, Sonali and I said "our mission is over' in unison. The Sun directed us, "our mission is not over, throw the serpents emerald in the mirror well so that none of the venom affects us". So, we calmly went and threw it in the transparent yet shiny mirror well.

The armor disappeared.

Chapter XVIII: Celebrations

In an instance we were returning safely back again in a much easier route. Shriyan invited us to the palace and to visit his land, palace, and people. We asked him about his father. He said he would have already reached the palace with his people and Shriyan was travelling slowly because we earthlings cannot travel fast. My mother urged that we return home back and visit them later as dads were alone back there.

As the mothers talked to Shriyan on the way back, my sister was joyfully playing with Corvi who joined us to say hello. She was asking if Corvi went to school and liked online classes or in-person lessons. Corvi answered everything in her own way and giggled some too. Sonali and I had one last question to which we didn't know the answer. We wished either the moon or Canopus would appear, and we could ask.

Right then a loud but clear voice came, "The Serpent wanted power, it was a matter of greed. He used all of these creatures as part of that plan by luring them with greed for power as well!

But in reality, he wanted infinite power so the serpent world will be most powerful, also known as Saturn in earthling world, also the reason we were involved is, because looks like one of our ancestors from a long time ago came here and before he could leave, he decided he liked that place. He thought it would be easy to communicate but something went wrong, and it wasn't possible until a few months ago."

Our question was cleared. Then Shriyan reminded us about the invite, we told him we would come for summer break.

¨Hey I know your houses is wrecked because restoring the emerald causes a huge accident but of course it doesn't hurt earthlings, but I have a fixing magical golden dust that will fix everything. Also, since there was unbalance here the time stopped there so nobody will know that it happened except the ones you told. ¨ Shriyan told us in a relieved voice.

¨Thanks for everything¨ I said, I was grateful to have such great friends. Snowbright enjoyed for a bit now that there was no pressure, she glided and dipped as she soared through the skies, it almost seemed like she was smiling.

When we reached our earthly home we parked Snowbright, after the emerald was restored in the correct place, time resumed so it was 10:45 pm when we reached. I was happy, looked like nobody could see Shriyan or anything from the other dimension and I guess they couldn't except other than our family, and looked like we were cousins too! I felt proud, like Sonali, Shriyan and I were a superhero team, but for real, not in fairy tales or cartoons or even movies because this is real.